MLA Index and Bibliography Series
Linda I. Solow, Editor

SPECULUM:

An Index of Musically Related Articles and Book Reviews

Second Edition

by
Arthur S. Wolff

Philadelphia
Music Library Association Inc.

Library of Congress Cataloging in Publication Data
Main entry under title:

Speculum : an index of musically related articles and
    book reviews.

    (MLA index and bibliography series ; 9 ISSN 0094-
6478)
    1. Music--History and criticism--Medieval--Bibliogra-
phy. 2. Speculum--Indexes. I. Wolff, Arthur S.
II. Series.
ML128.M3S6 1981   780'.902   81-11302
ISBN 0-914954-26-1   AACR2

MLA Index and Bibliography Series Number 9

ISBN: 0-914954-26-1
ISSN: 0094-6478

Printed in the United States of America

PREFACE

This updated and revised index facilitates quick location of all material relevant to the art of music culled from articles, reviews, reports, notes, memorials, and bibliographies contained in *Speculum, a Journal of Medieval Studies* from Volume 1, 1926 through Volume 54, 1979.

Numbered entries are for articles in *Speculum* arranged by their authors and for monographs, essays, musical editions, etc. reviewed therein arranged by their authors, editors, or titles as appropriate. Each numbered entry includes the full citation. (Thirty-five entries are later additions and are accommodated by the addition of lower-case letters.) All other entries serve as references from subjects, titles, catchword-titles, and reviewers' names to numbered entries. Each full bibliographic citation includes volume (year):page number.

Examples of the various kinds of entries follow:

118 Hewitt, Helen, *Harmonice musices odhecaton A.* Rev.: H. Leichtentritt, 18 (1943):124-27	Review of Hewitt's edition
119 Hibberd, Lloyd, "Estampie and Stantipes," 19 (1944):222-49	Article
Hibberd, Lloyd (reviewer), 146, 216; (subject), 201	Reviewer's name: as reviewer of books entered as 146 and 216; as subject in article 201
hymn, 4, 21, 175...; Byzantine, 44, 65...	Subject: as such in articles 4, 21, 175, etc,; as qualified subject in 44, 65, etc.

While many articles treat musical subjects exclusively, others vary widely in musical interest. A number of studies, though exemplary in substance, relate to music or to some aspect of musical scholarship in an ancillary or incidental way: Gumbert and Pope (codicology, diplomatics) 111, 191; Collins, Rudick, and Wall (dramaturgy, performance practice in plays) 61, 213, 238, 272; Blount (folk legend, place names) 30; Gransden (realistic observation) 108; Marshall (troubadour text editing) 149, 150; Meyer-Baer, Pacht, and Remnant (iconography) 154, 180, 205; Crane and Seebass (organology) 69, 227; Creed and Stevens (performance practice) 70, 241.

Other studies that mention music have been excluded from the index, however. These include the "beautiful horn sequence" in the *Chanson de Roland* where the hero sounds his oliphant on the battlefield of Roncevaux [Nichols, 44 (1969):51-77]; various monastic canons decreeing that the monks shall, among other duties, ritually sing or perform mass and office; a study of onomatopoeia in riddles and the "folkloristic belief that swans sang with their wings" [Nelson, 49 (1944):421-40]; the author who betrays "a tin ear for the music of Chaucer's irony" [Grennen, 49 (1974):158-59]; the lines *"Joy* is known, ranked around music" [Nitze, 29 (1954):698] or the whereabouts of the music to Fulbert of Chartres' hymn for peace during the eleventh-century peace movement [MacKinney, 5 (1930):181-206].

Also omitted are many nonmusical and specialized articles that, for instance, may relate to genres of poetry that are known to have been sung [i.e., the chanson de geste in the review of Belanger's *Damadien: The Religious Context of the French Epic* by R. J. Cormier, 52 (1977)]. On the other hand, Yerushalmi's review fails to mention whether Samelson's "Romances and Songs of Sephardim" contains music; therefore it was listed, though unnumbered.

Some brief notices of recent publications of musical interest that occur without critical treatment are also excluded from this index (i.e., Frederic L. Cheyette's notice of Cosman and Chandler, eds, *Machaut's World: Science and Art in the Fourteenth Century*. 54 (1979):882).

For their unselfish efforts in helping prepare the final copy, special acknowledgements are due Professor David Austin, Music Librarian; Dr. Walter J. Wentz; Kathy Wolff, Wichita State University; and Linda Solow, Music Librarian, The Libraries of the Massachusetts Institute of Technology.

Arthur S. Wolff
Wichita State University

Allen, Philip S. (reviewer), 244
Alma redemptoris Mater, Missa super (Power)/Apel (rev.), 77
Alram, 267
Alto gradu gloriae tollitur Tholosa (conductus), 271
Amalarius, 139
Ambitus, 268a
Ambrose, St., 201
Ambrosian Antiphonary, 211
Ambrosiaster, 139
Ambulatory and choir, 63, 278
American Musicological Society, 244a
Amicum quaerit (motet), 42
4 Amiet, Robert, *Repertorium Liturgicum Augustanum. Les témoins de la
     liturgie du diocèse d'Aoste, I, II.* Rev: C. Waddell, 52 (1977):341-43
Ammianus Marcellinus, 10
Amour et amicitia (poem), 195
Amours me fait désirer (Machaut, Ballade 36), 194
Amours mi font rejoir et non fin cuer (motet), 223
Anacrusis, 190
Analecta hymnica (Dreves), 60, 83, 133
Anaphora interstanzaic (musical identity), 233b
Andeli, Henri d', 81
Angelic chorus, 233; dancing, 154
Angels, 201
Angelus ad virginem (song), 97
Anglade, Joseph, 40
Anglès, Higini, 257a
5 Anglès, Higini, *El codex musical de las Huelgas.* Rev: H.P. Lattin,
     8 (1933):279-81
6 Anglès, Higini, *La música a Catalunya fins al segle XIII.*
     Rev: I. Pope, 12 (1937) 404-7
7 Anglès, Higini, *La música de las Cantigas de Santa María del Rey
     Alfonso el Sabio.* Rev: W. Apel, 22 (1947):458-60
Anima iugi/His hec, ratio/Caro, spiritui (triple motet), 223
Animal musicians, 1, 262
8 *Annales musicologiques: Moyen âge et Renaissance, I.* Rev: W. Apel,
     29 (1954):794-95
Annunciation, 284. *See also* Dramatic ceremonies (sacred).
Anonymous, 81, 201, 266
Anonymous IV, 81
Anonymous IV/Dittmer (rev.), 75; /Reckow (rev.), 203
Anonymous of St. Emmeram, 203
9 Anson, John S., "The Hunt of Love: Gottfried von Strassburg's Tristan
     as Tragedy," 45 (1970):594-607
Anthem, 163
9a *Antifonario Visigótico Mozárabe de la Catedral de León. Edicion
     facsimil.* Rev: W. Apel, 30 (1955):612-15
Antioche, La chanson d.'/Sumberg (rev.), 246
Antiphon, 20, 36, 45a, 47, 79, 83, 109, 123, 133, 213, 227, 238,
     244a, 272, 278
Antiphonale Sarisburiense, 60
Antiphonarium Mozarabicum de la Catedral de León/Padres
     Benedictino de Silo (rev.), 179

Antiphonary of Silos, 211
Antiphonary of Solesmes, 211
Antiphonary of Wamba at Leon, 179, 190, 192
Antiphons, Responsories and other Chants of the Mozarabic Rite/
    Brookett (rev.), 36
Antiphony, 17, 163
Antonio da Tempo, 119, 145, 147
Aostan liturgy, 4
10 Apel, Willi, "Early History of the Organ," 23 (1948):191-216
11 Apel, Willi, *French Secular Music of the Late Fourteenth Century.*
    Rev.: G. Haydon, 26 (1951):145-48
12 Apel, Willi, *Gregorian Chant.* Rev: S. Corbin, trans. by I. Pope,
    36 (1961):108-14
13 Apel, Willi, "Imitation Canons on *L'homme armé*," 25 (1950):367-73
   Apel, Willi (reviewer), 7 (Anglès), 8 (*Annales*), 9a (*Antifonario*),
       35 (Bragard), 41 & 43 (Bukofzer), 48 (Carapetyan), 64 (Connor),
       66 (Corbin), 75 (Dittmer), 77 (*D.P. Liturgicae*), 85 (*Études*),
       101, (Geering), 107 (*Graduel*), 143 (Machaut), 144 (McPeek),
       158 (Moberg), 161 & 164 (*M.M. Byzantinae*), 165 (*M.P. Liturgicae*),
       183 (Parrish), 204 (Reese), 221 & 222 (Schrade), 224 (Schuberth),
       247 (Sumner), 249 (Tappolet), 258 (Van), 263 (Verdeil), 268,269 &
       270 (Waesberghe)
14 Apfel, Ernst, *Studien zur Satztechnik der mittelalterlichen
    englischen Musik.* Rev: L.A. Dittmer, 36 (1961):443-47
   Aphrodite, 34
   Apocalypse, 151
   Apollo, 1, 201
15 Appel, Carl, *Die Singweisen Bernarts von Ventadorn.* Rev: H.R.
    Bitterman, 9 (1934):446
   Appel, Carl (subject), 40
   Aquinus, Thomas, 188
   Aquitanian introit trope, 86; notation, 167, 211
   Arbor scientarium, 239
   Architectura (Vitruvius), 10
   Aretinus, Guido, 39
   Aria, 142
   Arion and the dolphins, 201
   Aristoteles, Lambertus (Magister Lambert), 42, 271
   Aristotle, 40, 201
   Arithmetical theory, 103
16 Arlt, Wulf, *Ein Festoffizium des Mittelalters aus Beauvais in seiner
    liturgischen und musikalischen Bedeutung. I: Darstellungsband &
    II: Editionsband.* Rev: H. Tischler, 47 (1972):742-43
17 Arlt, Wulf, Ernst Lichtenhahn, and Hans Oesch, eds., *Gattungen der
    Musik in Einzeldarstellungen: Gedenkschrift Leo Schrade 1.*
    Rev: K.J. Levy, 52 (1977):915-16
18 Arnaud, L.E., "The *Sottes Chansons* in MS Douce 308 of the Bodleian
    Library at Oxford," 19 (1944):68-88
   Arnaud de Prat, 83
   Arnobius, 139
   Aron, Pietro, 42
   Ars antiqua, 123, 188
   Ars cantus mensurabilis (Franco of Cologne), 81

Ars musica, 81, 270a
Ars nova, 173
"*Art de dictier*, Deschamps' and Chaucer's Literary Environment"/
    Olson, 174
Art music, 119
19 *Arte pensiero e cultura a Mantova nel primo Rinacimento in rapporto
    con la Toscana e con il Veneto: Atti de VI convegno internazionale
    di studi sul Rinacimento. Firenze-Venezia-Mantova, 28 Settembre-
    1 Ottobre, 1961* (Istituto Nazionale di Studi sul Rinascimento).
    Rev: N.S. Streuver, 42 (1967):510-11
Arthurianum onomasticon (Blount), 30
Arundel, Archbishop of Canterbury, 29
Asaph 196, 227
Ascend, 152
Asclepiades, 201
Asini (joyful feast of subdeacons: Feast of the Ass), 16
Asinus ad lyam (Phaedrus), 1
Ass and the Harp, 1; Song of the, 109
Assonance, 188
Assumption (dramatic pageant), 284
Athanasius, 201
Athenaeus, 10
Atkinson, Charles M. (reviewer), 268a, 269a, 270a
Attently, 152
Au bois de Deuil (chanson), 90
Aubades, 217
Aubry, Pierre, 119
Auctoritas, 42
Audi chorum organicum (hymn), 10
Augustanum, Repertorium Liturgicum/Amiet (rev.), 4
Augustine, St., 10, 81, 130, 197, 198
Aulos, 201
Aurelian of Réome, 81, 123, 139, 275
Aurons Pfennig (minnesinger poem), 267
Authentic chants, 268a
Ave rex gentis Anglorum (sequence), 60
Avenary, Hanoch, 44
Aÿ deus se sab ora meu amigo (Codax), 190

B-fa and B-mi, 91
B.M.V., flight into Egypt, 109; presentation in the temple. 283
Babylonia, 1
Bacchus, 1
Bach, Johann Sebastian, 64
Bacon, Roger, 42, 81
Bagpipe, 29, 43a, 173, 262
20 Bailey, Terence, *The Processions of Sarum and the Western Church*.
    Rev: R.W. Pfaff, 48 (1973):337-239 [sic]
Baldwin, John W. (reviewer), 29a, 55
Ballad, 89
Ballad, Researches into the Mediaeval History of the Folk/Vargyas
    (rev.), 261
Balladas, 54

Canto misurato, Anonimi notitia del valore delle note/Carapetyan
(rev.), 48
Cantor, 10
Cantorales (Cisneros), 192
Cantus, 119
Cantus lamentationum (I-IV), 211
Canzona, 119, 147; etymology, 145
Canzoniere (Petrarch), 279
Capella, Martianus, 271
Capitals, ambulatory, 63, 278
48 Carapetyan, Armen, *Anonimi notitia del valore delle note del canto
misurato*. Rev: W. Apel, 33 (1958):382-83
49 Carghill, Oscar, *Drama and Liturgy*. Rev: G.R. Coffman, 4 (1931):
610-17, incl. bibliography
Caribus, 119
Carillon, 173
Carmen figuratum, 10; pastorale, 131
Carmina (Prophyrius), 10
Carmina burana, 125, 131, 235
Carminum, 83
Caro spiritui (conductus), 223
Carol, 89, 110a, 272, 276
Carole (chain dance), 119
Carolingian liturgy, 4; modal classification, 123; period, 96
Carols, The Early English/Greene (rev.), 110
Carols, Mediaeval/Stevens (rev.), 240
Caron, F., *Missa super L'homme armé/Monumenta polyphoniae liturgicae*
(rev.), 165
Caron, Philippe (Firmin), 13
Carpenter, Nan Cooke, 272
50 Carpenter, Nan Cooke, "Music in the *Secunda Pastorum*,"
26 (1951):696-700
Casella da Pistoia, 145
Casnac, Bernat de, 209
Cassiodorus, 10, 39, 81; glossary, 139; influence and dissemination
of resources, 128, 129
Castilian poets, religious song, 190
Castilian Verse, Fifteenth Century, Morphology of/Clarke (rev.), 57
Catalunya, La musica a, fins al segle XIII/Anglès (rev.), 6
Cauda, 226
51 Cavallo, Guglielmo, *Rotoli di Exultet dell'Italia Meridionale:
Exultet 1, 2, Benedizionale dell'Archivio della Cattedrale di Bari,
Exultet 1, 2, 3 dell'Archivio Capitolare di Troia*. Rev: G.B.
Ladner, 51 (1976):720-22
52 Celli-Fraentzel, Anna, "Contemporary Reports on the Medieval Roman
Climate," 7 (1932):96-106
Celtic musical forms, 256
Centonizing, 83
Cercamon, 131
Chailley, Jacques, ed., *Messe Notre Dame*/Machaut (rev.), 143
Chain dance, 119
53 Chamberlain, David S., "Philosophy of Music in the *Consolatio* of
Boethius," 45 (1970):80-97

53a Chambers, E.K., *The English Folk-Play*. Rev: G.R. Coffman,
   10 (1935):203-5
 54 Chambers, Frank M., *Proper Names in the Lyrics of the Troubadours*.
   Rev: N. Iliescu, 49 (1974):105-6
Chanson, 142b, 145, 169a, 174, 260; amoureuses, 18, 140; Burgundian,
   44; de femme, 21b; de geste, 62, 80, 93, 94, 105, 126, 127, 131
   215, 220, 245; de mal mariée, 131; dramatique, 131; French, 21b,
   44, 233b; pastourelle, 131; sources, 90
Chanson Albums of Marguerite of Austria/Picker (rev.), 187
La chanson d'Antioche/Sumberg (rev.), 246
Chanson de Roland, 80, 126, 215, 220
Chansonnier, 199
Chansonnier Cangé, 145, 260
Chansonnier Provençal, 230
Chansonniers des troubadours et des trouvères/Beck (rev.), 22
Chansons de geste du cycle de Guillaume d'Orange/Frappier (rev.),
   93,94
Chansons latines (motets), 223
Chansos, 54
Chant. *See* Authentic chants; Byzantine chant; Gregorian chant; Mozarabic
   chant; Plagal chants; Proper chant; Responsorial chant; Slavic music
Chant Grégorien/Bescond (rev.), 25
Charité, 18
Charlemagne, 27, 52, 224
Charles the Bald, coronation, 96
Chartres Fragment, 244a
Chase, 193, 251
Chastity, 273
Chaucer, Geoffrey, 1, 29, 60, 96, 173, 174, 193, 194, 273
Cheironomiai, 65
 55 Cheney, C.R., "The Diocese of Grenoble in the Fourteenth Century,"
   10 (1935):162-77
Chester Cycle, 151
Chifonie, 173
Chilston, 39, 152
Chimes, 173
China, 42
Chlodwig (Clovis I; also Hlodowig, Frankish king), 224
Chobham, Thomas de, "Summa Confessorum" (rev.), 29a
Choir and ambulatory, 63, 278
Choral vs. soloist music, 272
Chorister's Lament, 58, 91, 257
Choses tassin (instrumental dance), 119
Chretien de Troyes, 142b
Christ ist erstanden (hymn), 124
Christian allegory, 42; doctrine of music, 40
Christian Rite and Christian Drama in the Middle Ages/Hardison
   (rev.), 114
Christus manens (chant, organum triplum), 119, 122
Christus surrexit (antiphon; triumphal march), 192
Chrysostum, St. John, 28
Church fronts, 1; choir and ambulatory, 278. *See also*
   Modes, Gregorian

Ciati, Simone, 147
Cicero, 10, 201
Circumcision (Feast of), 122
Cisneros, Cardinal Francisco Ximenez de, 192, 211
Cithara, 42, 119, 191, 201
Cithern, 196
Citole, 173
Clarion, 173
56 Clark, J.M., *The Abbey of St. Gall as a Centre of Literature and Art*. Rev: E.K. Rand, 2 (1927):354-56
57 Clarke, Dorothy C., *Morphology of Fifteenth Century Castilian Verse*. Rev: E.B. Place, 39 (1964):508-10
Claudianus, Claudius, 10
Clausula, 42, 122, 188, 257; textual, 226
Clavechord, 173
Clavicin, 173
Clavicymbal, 173
Clements, Robert J. (reviewer), 58
Cloches (bells), 173
Close, 152
Cluny, 106; ambulatory capitals, 63, 278
Coblas, 54, 119; singulars, 226
Codax, Martim, 190
Codex. *See* Manuscripts; names of specific codices
Codicology, 111
Coffman, George R. (reviewer), 49, 53a, 282
58 Cohen, Gustave, *La vie littéraire en France au moyen âge*. Rev: R.J. Clements, 29 (1954):795-96
Colby-Hall, Alice (reviewer), 105, 245
Collect, 211
59 *Collectanea Vaticana in honorem Anselmi M. Card. Albareda a Bibliotheca Apostolica edita*. Rev: Anon., 39 (1964):576
Collegerunt pontifices (antiphon), 213
60 Collins, Fletcher, "The Kings Note, The Miller's Tale, Line 31," 8 (1933):195-97
Collins, Fletcher, 272
61 Collins, Fletcher, Jr., *The Production of Medieval Church Music-Drama*. Rev: G. Frank, 48 (1973):738-40
Collins, H.S. Frank (reviewer), 255
62 Colliot, Regine, *Adenet le Roi*, Berte aus grans piés, *Étude littéraire générale, I, II*. Rev: J. Gildea O.S.A., 46 (1971):137-39
Comedy, 245
La Commedia (Dante), 188
Commercia modorum, 10
Common of Virgins, 272
Commune sanctorum (Spanish), 211
Communion, 227, 259, 278
Como vivo coitada (poem, pilgrimage song), 190
Compendium musices (Lampadius), 272
Compensation (for loss of hands), 142a
Complaincte, 90
Compline, 16
Composition (musical), intellectual purpose, 42; rules, 271

Couple dance, 119
Court de Paradis, Poème. anonyme du XIIIe siècle/Vilamo-Pentti
    (rev.), 266
Coussemaker, Charles-Edmond-Henri de, 81, 202, 203, 223, 271
Crab canon, 42
Crack, 50
Craft cycles, 272
Craig, Hardin, 238
69 Crane, Frederic, *Extant Medieval Musical Instruments: A Provisional
    Catalogue by Types.* Rev: E.A. Bowles, 49 (1974):324-26
Cranz, F. Edward (reviewer), 134
70 Creed, Robert P., ed., *Old English Poetry: Fifteen Essays.* Rev:
    F.C. Robinson, 45 (1970):283-89
Crocker, Richard L., 132
Cromorne (douceine), 173
71 Cropp, Glynnis M., *Le vocabulaire courtois des troubadours de l'époque
    classique.* Rev: D. Kelly, 52 (1977):945-47
Croxton Play, 233
Crusader's song, 186
Cserba, Simon M., 188
Ctesibius, 10, 28
Cuckoo, 1
Cum esset in accubitu (responsory), 83
Cummins, Patricia W. (reviewer), 21b
Cunsette, 152
Curriculum requirements at Oxford, 81
Cursus, 228
Cycles, French, of the Ordinarium Missae/Schrade, *Polyphonic Music
    of the Fourteenth Century* (rev.), 221
Cymbala/Waesberghe (rev.), 268
Cymbala ad cantandum, 253
Cymbals, 173, 264
Cyrille, St., 218
Cythara Teutonica, 191. *See also* Kithara
Cywydd-metre, 151a

D'Accone, Frank A. (reviewer), 265
72 Dahlberg, Charles, "Love and the *Roman de la Rose*," 44 (1969):568-84
Dance, 53a, 119, 273; song, 79, 276
Dancing angels, 154
Daniel play, 61, 122, 238
Dansa, 54, 119
Dante Alighieri, 145, 188
Danza, 273
Data processing, musical, 44
David, 201, 227; with the harp, 1
73 Davis, Norman, ed., *Non-Cycle Plays and Fragments.* Rev: D.
    Bevington, 46 (1971):733-36
De amicita (Cicero), 195
De anima (Tertullian), 10
De arithmetica (Boethius), 53

Dum trahit vehicula (motet), 109
D'une niepce sur la mort de sa tante (Marot), 90
Dunn, E. Catherine, 250
Dunstable, John, 42, 50, 272
Dunstable, John, Complete Works/Bukofzer (rev.), 41
Dunstan, St., 28, 106
Dupla, 254
Duplex longa, 254
Durrenmatt, H.R., 44

Early Celtic Versecraft/Travis (rev.), 256
Early English Carols, The/Greene (rev.), 110; 2nd ed. (rev.), 110a
Early Trope Repertory of Saint Martial de Limoges/Evans (rev.), 86
Easter hymns, 124, 280; Holy Week, 4; Introit and Mass, 284;
    plays, 32, 78, 98a, 124, 213, 238, 242, 280, 284; sequence, 175;
    trope, 238; vespers, 32
Eastern Elements in Western Chant/Wellesz (rev.), 162
Échecs amoureux (anonymous), 173
Eclogues (Virgil), 201
Edda (Elder), 142
80a Egbert, Donald Drew, "The 'Tewkesbury' Psalter," 10 (1935):376-86
Eight modes. *See* Modes, Gregorian
Eighth, 152
Ekkehard IV, 226
Ele·(panpipes), 173
Eleanor of Aquitaine, 21a
"*Elene 1-113*, Themes and Type-Scenes in"/Fry, 98
81 Ellingwood, Leonard, "Ars Musica," 20 (1945):290-99
82 Ellingwood, Leonard, *The Works of Francesco Landini*. Rev: J.-B.
    Beck, 15 (1940):503-7
Ellingwood, Leonard (reviewer), 148, 240, 281
Eman, 227
Embellishment, 119, 241
Emmaus (story), 98a
Emmeram Anonymous, St., 271
Emotions, 201
Enarrationes in psalmos (Augustine), 10
Enchiridion, 44
Encontre le tens de pascour/Mens fidem seminat (motet), 223
England, 108; liturgical music, 78, 130, 205; manuscripts, 134a;
    treatises, 152
England, New Liturgical Feasts in Later Medieval/Pfaff (rev.), 185
Englischen Mittelalter, Hymnar und Hymnen/Greuss (rev.), 106
Englischen Musik, Studien zur Satztechnik der mittelalterlichen/
    Apfel (rev.), 14
English Advent, The Old/Burlin (rev.), 45
English Art, A Study of the Fox in/Varty (rev.), 262
English Carols, The Early/Greene (rev.), 110
English Drama, Medieval/Taylor (rev.), 250
English Folk Play/Chambers (rev.), 53a
English Poetry, Old/Creed (rev.), 70

Felix regnum (Responsories 1 & 2 for Matins), 83
Felix spina (responsory), 83
Fiddle, 196
Fidibus, 10
Fifteenth, 152
Fifth, 152
Finalis, 83, 268a
Finis clausulae and punctorum, 203
Fischer, Hans, 124, 217
Fischer, Kurt von, 188
Fisher, John H. (reviewer), 251
Fletcher, J.M. (editor), 177
Florentine chapels ca. 1475-1525, 265
Floresbit (clausula) of the organum *Alleluya, justus germinabit*, 223
Flute, 1, 173
Folk Ballad, Researches into the Mediaeval History of/Vargyas
   (rev.), 261
Folksong, 89
88 Ford, J.D.M., Kenneth McKenzie, and George Sarton, "Memoir,
   Jean-Baptiste Beck," 19 (1944):384-85
Ford, J.D.M. (reviewer), 126
Forest (composer), 272
Form, 196a, 260
Formes fixes. *See* Ballade; Rondeau; Virelai
Fors seulement (chanson), 90
Fortunatus, Venantius, 10, 138
Fountains Fragment, 272
Fourteenth Century Italian Cacce/Marrocco, 146
89 Fowler, David C., *A Literary History of the* Popular Ballad.
   Rev: A.B. Friedman, 45 (1970):127-29
Fox, Denton (reviewer), 95
Foxes with musical instruments, 262
France, 11, 21b, 38, 40, 58, 78, 112, 221
Francesco da Barbarino, 145, 147
Franco of Cologne, 42, 81, 203, 271
90 Françon, Marcel, "Clément Marot and Popular Songs," 25 (1950):247-48
91 Françon, Marcel, "Notes on the Use of the Guidonian Nomenclature by
   Machaut and Rabelais," 22 (1947): 249-50
92 Françon, Marcel, "Rondeaux Tercets," 24 (1949):88-92
Françon, Marcel (reviewer), 93
Frank, Grace (reviewer), 2, 38, 61
Frantzen, J.J.A.A., 131
Frappièr, Jean, 21b, 214
93 Frappièr, Jean, *Les chansons de geste du cycle de Guillaume d'Orange*.
   Rev: M. Françon, 31 (1956):508
94 Frappièr, Jean, *Les chansons de geste du cycle de Guillaume d'Orange,
   II: le Couronnement de Louis, le Charroi de Nimes, la Prise d'Orange*.
   Rev: C.M. Jones, 42 (1967):736-39
Frauenlob (Heinrich von Meissen), 267
Freccero, John, 188
Freiburg, University, The Mediaeval Statutes of the Faculty of Arts/
   Ott and Fletcher (rev.), 177

French Secular Music of the Late Fourteenth Century/Apel (rev.), 11
French Secular Theater, Music in/Brown (rev.), 38
Frere, W.H., 60
Frestal (panpipes), 173
Friderich von Husen, 166
Friedman, Albert B. (reviewer), 89
95 Friedman, John Block, *Orpheus in the Middle Ages*. Rev: D. Fox,
    48 (1973):141-42
Friedman, Lionel J. (reviewer), 80
Friedrich, 267
96 Friend, Albert M., Jr., "Two Manuscripts of the School of St.
    Denis," 1 (1926):59-70
Froissart, Jean, 21a, 119
Fromm, Hans, 217
97 Frost, George L., "The Music of *The Kinges Note*," 8 (1933):526-28
98 Fry, Donald K., "Themes and Type-Scenes in *Elene 1-113*," 44 (1969):35-45
Fulgentius, 42
Fulget signis (rex) (responsory), 83

Gabrieli, Goivanni, 119
Gadd, C.J., 1
Gafori, Franchino, 42
Gaius, 201
Galaveris, George (reviewer), 169
Galician lyric, 190; poetry, 135
Gallo, F. Alberto, 188
Gamut, 152
Garcia, Juan, de Castrojerez, 273
98a Gardiner, Frank Cook, *The Pilgrimage of Desire: A Study of Theme and
    Genre in Medieval Literature*. Rev: S.A. Barney, 48 (1973):359-62
99 Gardner, John, *The Alliterative "Morte Arthure, The Owl and the
    Nightingale,"* and *Five Other Middle English Poems in a Modernized
    Version with Comments on Poems and Notes*. Rev: T.H. Bestul,
    48 (1973):142-46
Garin le Loherain, Le style epique dans/Gittleman (rev.), 105
Gascoigne, George, 201
100 Gathercole, Patricia M., *Tension in Boccaccio: Boccaccio and the Fine
    Arts*. Rev: B.J. Layman, 52 (1977):676-78
Gaudate populi (antiphon), 192
Gaude Maria, 122
Gaude mater ecclesia (hymn), 83
Gaude regnum francie (antiphon), 83
Gaydon, chanson de geste, Étude sur/Subrenat (rev.), 245
Gedrut, 267
101 Geering, Arnold, *Die Organa und mehrstimmigen Conductus in den
    Handschriften des deutschen Sprechgebiets vom 13. bis 16.
    Jahrhundert*. Rev: W. Apel, 29 (1954):803
Gemeindelied, 124
Genius (priest), 72
Gennrich, Friedrich, *Die altfranzosische Rotronenge (1925)*, 21b
Georgiades, Thrasybulos, 39
Georgics, 131

Grammar, Old Provençal, 149; Latin, 210
Grandgent, C.H. (reviewer), 22
108 Grandsen, Antonia, "Realistic Observation in Twelfth Century England,"
    47 (1972):29-51
Grave, Salverda de, 131
109 Greene, Henry Copley, "The Song of the Ass; *Orientis Partibus* with
    special reference to Egerton MS 2615," 4 (1931):534-49
Greene, Richard L., 276
110 Greene, Richard L., ed., *The Early English Carols*. Rev: G.H.
    Gerould, 11 (1936):298-300
110a Greene, Richard L., ed., *The Early English Carols*. Second Edition
    revised and enlarged. Rev: S. Wenzel, 54 (1979):140-42
Gregorian Antiphonary of Silos, 211
Gregorian chant, 42, 96, 101, 198, 271, 278; in Bach, 64; in
    England, 130. *See also* Plainchant
Gregorian Chant/Apel (rev.), 12
Grégorien, Le chant/Bescond (rev.), 25
Grégorienne, Introduction à la paléographie musicale/Suñol
    (rev.), 248
Grégoriennes, Études (rev.), 85
Gregory the Great, St., 42, 96, 130, 188, 213
Grimm, Wilhelm, 217
Guido d'Arezzo, 10, 81, 123, 269a, 278
Guidonian nomenclature, 91, 152, 236
Guidonis Aretini, Expositiones in Micrologum/Waesberghe (rev.), 269
Guidonis Aretini Micrologus/Waesberghe (rev.), 270
Guillaume d'Orange, 93, 94
Guillem de Berguedà/Riquer (rev.), 209
Guiraut de Bornelh, 40, 233b
Guiraut de Cavera, 246
111 Gumbert, J.P., *Die Utrechter Kartäuser und ihre Bücher im frühen
    fünfzehnten Jahrhundert*. Rev: R.B. Marks, 52 (1977):685-87
Gunzo, 278
Gustate et uidete (antiphon), 192
Gymel, 272

Habel, Edwin, 271
Habitabit confidenter (antiphon), 83
Hack (division, ornamentation), 50
Hagiography and music, 133
Hainaut (court of Count William I), 206
112 Hamlin, Frank R., Peter T. Rickets, John Hathaway, eds., *Introduction
    à l'étude de l'ancien provençal*. Rev: S.G. Nichols, Jr.,
    44 (1969):137-40
Hamm, Charles, 83
Hammers, Reinhold, 53
Hanboys, John, 50
Handlo, Robert de, 42, 50, 119, 223
Handlo, Roberto de/Dittmer (rev.), 75
Handschin, Jacques, 188, 223
113 Hanford, James Holly, "The Progenitors of Golias," 1 (1926):38-58
Hanford, James Holly (reviewer), 3, 76
Hansen, F.E., 44

His hec racio (motet), 223
Historia: Études sur la genèse des offices versifiés/
    Jonsson (rev.), 133
120a *History and Cultural Contribution of the Jews of Spain and Portugal.*
    I: The Jews in Spain and Portugal before and after the Expulsion
    of 1493, W. Samelson: "Romances and Songs of the Sephardim."
    Rev: Y.H. Yerushalmi, 48 (1973):730-31
Hjálmar's Death-Song, 142
Hlodowig (Frankish king; also Chlodowig), 224
Hocket, 271; hoquetus, 202
Hodie scietis (Introit), 278
Höeg, Carsten, 244a
Höeg, Carsten, *La notation ekphonétique/Monumenta musicae byzantinae*
    (rev.), 160
Höeg, Carsten, ed., *Sticherarium/Monumenta musicae byzantinae*
    (rev.), 160
Hoepffner, Ernest, 174
Hoger of Werden, 138
Hohenfels, Burkhart von, 267
Hollander, John, 53, 142a
Holmes, Urban T., Jr. (reviewer), 140, 149, 246, 266
Holy Communion, Office for, 259
Holy Week, 4. *See also* Easter
L'homme armé, canons, 13; Mass, 165
Hoquetus, 202; hocket, 271
Horn, 173, 193, 264
Hornblower, 108
Hornbostel, Eric von, 69
Hornpipe (instrument), 173
Hosanna filio David (antiphon), 213
Hucbald, 28, 123
Hudson, Barton, 44
*Huelgas, El codex musical de las/*Anglès (rev.), 5
Hugh of Cluny, St., 278
Hughes, Andrew, 83
121 Hughes, Andrew, *Medieval Music: The Sixth Liberal Art.* Rev: T.H.
    Connolly, 52 (1977):381-82
122 Hughes, David G., "Liturgical Polyphony at Beauvais in the Thirteenth
    Century," 34 (1959):184-200
Hughes, David G. (reviewer), 86, 202, 203
123 Huglo, Michel, *Les tonaires. Inventaire, analyse, comparaison.*
    Rev: K.J. Levy, 49 (1974):125-26
Huglo, Michel (subject), 268a
Hugo (Hugh) of St. Victor, 233a, 271
Hugo von Trimberg, 1
Hull, Vernam E., 204a
Hunc natura (responsory), 83
Huon d'Oisy, 142b
Hurdy-gurdy, 173
Hus, Jan, 159
*Hüsen, Friderich von/*Mowatt (rev.), 166
Husmann, Heinrich, 188
Hydraulis, 10, 28, 139, 260

Intrando ad abitar (Gherardello da Firenze), 147
Introductio de musica mensurabili (Garlandia), 271
Introduction à l'étude de l'ancien provençal/Hamlin (rev.), 112
Introit, 192, 227, 274, 278; trope, 86
Invocantem exaudivit (antiphon), 83
Iod. Manum suam misit hostis (antiphon), 211
Irish music, 204a
Isidorus of Seville, 81
Islam, 121
Istampita, 119
Italian music, 146, 147, 148, 233a, 265
123a Ives, Samuel A., "A Rhymed Latin Poem on the Seven Arts,"
17 (1942):416-17

Jacobi Leodiensis speculum musicae/Bragard (rev.), 35
Jacobus de Voragine, *Legenda aurea*, 272
Jacobus of Liége, 42, 81
Jacopo da Bologna, 145, 147
Jacopo da Bologna, The Music of/Marrocco (rev.), 148
Jacopo da Forli, 233a
Jacques de Cambrai, 209a
Jaeschki, Hilde, 40
James, St., 16
Jammers, Ewald, 133
Janota, Johannes, 238
124 Janota, Johannes, *Studien zu Funktion und Typus des deutschen
geistlichen Liedes im Mittelalter.* Rev: E. Simon, 45 (1970):302-4
Jarcho, Boris I., 198
125 Jarcho, Boris I., "Die Vorläufer des Golias," 3 (1928):523-79
*Jaufré, Rudel, L'amour lointain de, et le sens de la poësie des
troubadours*/Spitzer (rev.), 237
Jay tout perdu mon tempts et mon labour (chanson), 173
Jean Bodel, Les Congés d'Arras/Ruelle (rev.), 214
Jean de Condé, 119; *Jean de Condé*/Ribard (rev.), 206, 207
Jean de Lescurel, 109
Jean le Teinturier d'Arras, 81
Jeanne d'Evreux, Hours of, 199
Jeanroy, Alfred, 40, 131
126 Jenkins, T.A., *La Chanson de Roland.* Rev: J.D.M. Ford, 2 (1927):92-104
Jensen, Kenneth (reviewer), 176
Jerome, St., 139, 271
Jerome of Moravia, 81, 83, 114, 188, 271
Jeu-parti, 18
Job xxxviii, 37, 201
Joculator, 113
Jofre de Foixa, 150
Johannes de Garlandia, 81, 131, 174, 203, 271
Johannes de Grocheo, 42, 81, 119, 145, 173
John Chrysostom, St., 28
John of Seville, 188
127 Jones, C. Meredith, "The Conventional Saracen of the Songs of
Geste, " 17 (1942):201-25

Kithara, 42, 119, 191, 201
Klapper, Joseph, 284
Des Knaben Wunderhorn, 217
Knack (division), 50
Kolmarer Liederhandschrift, 38a
Königsteiner Liederbuch/Sappler (rev.), 217
Kontakion, 17, 244a
Krappe, A.H., 1
136 Kraus, Carl von, *Walther von der Vogelweide und die Gedichte
    Walthers von der Vogelweide*. Rev: C. Selmer, 14 (1939):127
Krov' tvoia (troparion), 259
Krumhorn, 173
137 Kuhn, Hugo, *Minnesangs Wende*. Rev: H. Adolf, 29 (1954):293-95
138 *Kulturhistorisk leksikon for nordisk middelalder fra vikingetid til
    reformationstid, X: Kyrloratt-Ludus de Sancto Canuto Duce*. Rev: L.S.
    Thompson, 41 (1966):549-50
Kushner, Eva, 142a

La Clayette Manuscript, 223
138a La Piana, George, "The Byzantine Theater," 11 (1936):171-211
La Rue, Pierre de, 13
Ladino, 120a
Ladner, Gerhart B. (reviewer), 51
Laetabundus (Christmas sequence), 16
Lai, 17 21a, 54, 142, 142a, 142b, 156, 202, 206, 226; -sequence, 119, 235
Lais des Jacobins et des Fremeneurs, 206
Laisse, 235
139 Laistner, M.L.W., "The Mediaeval Organ and a Cassiodorus Glossary
    among the Spurious Works of Bede," 5 (1930):217-21
Lambert, Magister, 42, 271
Lambert, St., 10
Lambeth Psalter, 106
Lament, 257
Lament of the Choristers, 257
Lamentations de Matheolus, 173
Lamentations of Jeremiah, 192, 211
Lampadius, *Compendium musices*, 272
Landini, Francesco, 145, 147
Landini, Francesco, The Works of/Ellingwood (rev.), 82
Langfors, Arthur, 81
140 Langfors, Arthur, *Deux recueils de sottes chansons: Bodleienne
    Douce 308 et Bibliothèque Nationale Fr. 24432*. Rev: U.T. Holmes
    Jr., 22 (1947):651-52
Langohr, 1
Lansberg, H., 132
Lascelle, Joan, 69
Last Judgement, 238
Last Supper, 199, 213, 238
Latin, grammar, 210; hymnody, 175; liturgical drama, 32, 280; Love
    songs, 131, 234; minstrels, 113; poetry, 173, 195, 217, 226, 229;
    sequence, 98a, 142c, 190, 195, 235
Latin Lyrics, Mediaeval/Allen (rev.), 3
Latin Songs and Satires, The Goliard Poets/Whicher (rev.), 277

Liturgique, Le deposition du Christ, au vendredi saint/Corbin (rev.), 66
Liturgischen Hymnen in Schweden/Moberg (rev.), 158
Liturgy, Carolingian, 4; eleventh century, 16, 109; Marian, 272;
    reforms, 159; Russian, 259; thirteenth century, 122; use of
    organ in, 224
Llanthony Priory, 37a
Lockwood, Lewis, 44
142 Lönnroth, Lars, "Hjálmar's Death-Song and the Delivery of Eddic
    Poetry," 46 (1971):1-20
Longa, 42, 241, 254
142a Louis, Kenneth R.R. Gros, "Robert Henryson's *Orpheus and Eurydice*
    and the Orpheus Traditions of the Middle Ages," 41 (1966):643-55
Louis VII, 254
Lovillo, J. Guerrero, 135
Lowinsky, Edward B., 272
Ludi Paschales (Easter play), 238
Ludovicus decus regnatium (antiphon), 83
Ludovicus dominum (antiphon), 83
Ludovicus hodie (antiphon), 83
Ludus Coventriae XXIII, 272
Ludus de Antichristo, 238
Ludwig, Friedrich, 123, 223
Lune Mercure Vénus Soleil Mars Jupiter Saturne (Nicomague), 34
Lusignan, Serge, 44
Lute, 43a, 173, 201, 204a; German tablature, 217
Lydian (mode), 278
Lyon, 4
Lyre, 201, 227; Sumarian, 1; Sutton Hoo, 191
Lyre Abbey, 196
Lyric, The Medieval/Dronke (rev.), 79
Lyric poetry, 54, 84, 121, 276; as natural music, 174; Galician, 135, 190
Lyrics, Religious, of the XIVth Century/Brown (rev.), 37

Ma fin est mon commencement (Machaut), 42
142b McCash, June Hall Martin, "Marie de Champagne and Eleanor of
    Aquitaine: A Relationship Reexamined," 54 (1979):698-711
McCulloch, Florence (reviewer), 156
142c McDonald, A.D., "The Iconographic Tradition of Sedulius,"
    8 (1933):150-56
Machabey, Armand, ed., *Messe Notre Dame*/Machaut (rev.), 143
Machaut, Guillaume de, 42, 46, 91, 92, 173, 174, 194
Machaut, Guillaume de/Reaney (rev.), 202
143 Machaut, Guillaume de, *Messe Notre Dame* (ed. by Jacques Chailley,
    d'Armand Machabey, and Guglielmus de Van). Rev: W. Apel, 26 (1951):
    187-90
Machaut, Guillaume de, The Works of/Schrade, *Polyphonic Music of*
    the Fourteenth Century (rev.), 222
McKenzie, Kenneth, 88
Maclean, Charles, 10
144 McPeek, Gwynn S., *The British Museum Manuscript Egerton 3307*.
    Rev: W. Apel, 39 (1964):728-29

Manuscripts, continued

Leyden, University Library, Scaliger Ms. 38b: 259

London, British Mus., Add. 5665 (Ritson): 272; Add. 16975: 196; Add. 19352: 169; Add. 27630: 122, 254; Add. 28550 (Robertsbridge Codex): 10, 119; Add. 29987: 119, 145; Add. 30072: 83; Add. 40011 B. (Fountains Fragment): 272

London, British Mus., Arundel 292: 257

London, British Mus., Egerton 274: 122; Egerton 2615 (Beauvais): 109, 122, 254; Egerton 2616: 16

London, *British Museum Manuscript Egerton 3307*/McPeek (rev.), 144

London, British Mus., Harley 978: 119; Harley 5589: 10

London, British Mus., Lansdowne 763: 39, 152

London, British Mus., Royal 8 B xiv: 146; Royal 13 B viii: 108

London, British Mus., Sloan 2593: 60

London, *Westminster Abbey 33327*/Dittmer (rev.), 75

Lucca, Bibl. capitolare, Ms. 603: 236

Madrid, Bibl. Nac. 192/Dittmer (rev.), 75

Madrid, B.N. 20486: 254

Milan, Bibl. Ambrosiana R 71 sup.: 82, 228, 236

Modena, Codex Estense Lat. 568: 147

Montpellier, Bib. de l'Ecole de Med. H 159: 192; H 196: 82, 223

Montpellier, Bib. de la Fac. de Med. H 196: 81, 199, 254

Munich, Staatsbibl., Cgm 4997: 38a; Clm 835: 196; Clm 5539: 235

Munich, Staatsbibl., lat. 3909 (Ordinarium): 283; lat. 4668: 122; lat 16444: 254

Naples, B.N. VII D 14: 268a

New York City, Pierpont Morgan Lib., Phillips: 40

Old Hall (Herts.), St. Edmonds College Old Hall Ms.: 272

Oxford   Bodleian Libr., Bodley 572: 236

Oxford, *Bodleian Library Douce 269, The Oxford Provencal Chansonnier : Diplomatic Edition of the Manuscript*/Shepard (rev.), 230

Oxford, Bodleian Libr., Douce 308: 18, 119, 140

Oxford, Corpus Christi College 59: 37a

Padua, Bibl. Capitulare, C55 and C56: 188; Fufu (Processionale): 283

Paris, B. n., f. fr. 146 (Roman de Fauvel): 122, 223, 254; f. fr. 844: 119, 223

Paris, *B.N., Fonds Francais, Manuscript du Rou No. 844*/Beck, 223; (rev.), 23

Paris, B.n., f. fr. 846 (Chansonnier Cangé): 81, 145, 260; f. fr. 12615: 223, 254; f. fr. 22543: 119

Paris, *Bibliotheque Nationale Fr. 24432, Deux recueils de sottes chansons*/Langfors (rev.), 140

Paris, B.n., f. ital. 568: 82, 145, 147

Paris, B.n., f. lat. 745: 83; f. lat. 746: 83; f. lat. 746a: 83; f. lat. 911: 83; f. lat. 1026: 83; f. lat. 1052: 83; f. lat. 1118: 227, 235; f. lat. 1121: 86; f. lat. 1139: 122, 254; f. lat. 1141: 96; f. lat. 1154: 235; f. lat. 2292: 96; f. lat. 3549: 254; f. lat. 3719: 235, 254; f. lat. 7202: 139; f. lat. 10525: 196; f. lat. 11550: 171; f. lat. 15139 (St. Victor 813): 188, 254

Paris, B.n., nouv. acq. fr. 13521: 223

Paris 13521 & 11411 (La Clayette)/Dittmer (rev.), 75

Pommersfelden, Frafl. Schonborn'sche Bibl. 2776: 10

152 Meech, Sanford B., "Three Fifteenth Century English Musical Treatises,"
    10 (1935):235-69
   Meistersinger, 38a; R. Wagner, 1
   Melia, Daniel F. (reviewer), 256
   Melisma, 86, 203
   Melodic analysis, 190, 233b, 244a, 250; embellishment, 119;
     identity, 233b
   Melodrama, 142
   Mendel, Arthur, 44
   Menestrellorum multitudo/Bullock-Davies (rev.), 43a
   Mensural vs. unmeasured notation, 257
   Mensuration canon, 13
   Mercury, 34
   Merrilees, Brian S. (reviewer), 206
   Mersenne, Marin, 81
   Mese, 34
   Messe des oiseaux, Jean de Condé/Ribard (rev.), 206
153 Messenger, Ruth Ellis, "Hymnista," 22 (1947):83-84
   Metamorphis goliae, 24
   Meter, 70, 151a, 260
   Mettmann, W., 135
   Metz, 96
   Meyer, Paul, 223
   Meyer, Wilhelm, 190, 195
154 Meyer-Baer, Kathi, *Music of the Spheres and the Dance of Death:*
     Studies in Musical Iconology. Rev: M.W. Bloomfield, 46 (1971):172-74
   Mia ŷrmana fremosa treidas (Codax), 190
   Micanon, 173
   Michael, Wolfgang F., 280
155 Michael, Wolfgang F., *Das deutsche Drama des Mittelalters.* Rev:
     E. Simon, 48 (1973):776-79
156 Mickel, Emanuel J., Jr., *Marie de France.* Rev: F. McCulloch,
     52 (1977):407-8
157"Microfilms and Photostats of European Manuscripts" [includes an
     important list of French Mss. destroyed during the War (1939-
     1945) and Italian libraries in which Mss. were destroyed, damaged,
     or lost], 29 (1954):336-38
   Micrologus (Guido), 10, 81
   Midas, 1
   Middle Ages, Music in the/Reese (rev.), 204
   Middle English (tract on proportions), 39
   Midsummer Night's Dream (Shakespeare), 1
   Miller's Tale (Chaucer), 29, 60, 96
   Miniatures, 135, 169, 196, 200
   Minnelieder, 217, 252
   Minnesänger, Trouvères und/Müller-Blattau (rev.), 168
   Minnesangs Wende/ Kuhn (rev.), 137
   Minnesinger, 119, 131, 166, 184, 196b, 232, 235, 252, 267
   Minstrels, 43a, 62, 69, 89, 142a, 207; bi- (or tri-) lingual, 178
   Miracle plays, 272
   Misericords, A Catalogue of, in Great Britain/Remnant (rev.), 205
   Missale mixtum (Cisneros), 192

(158-165)

Missals, 1, 192
Mixolydian (mode), 278
Moaxaha (Moorish), 190
158 Moberg, Carl Allen, *Die liturgischen Hymnen in Schweden, I:
Quellen und Texte. Text- und Melodieregister.* Rev: W.
Apel, 30 (1955):669-70
Modal analysis, 86; formulae, 83; rhythm, 42, 203, 260; scales, 260;
signatures, 65
Modena, soldiers' song, 219
Modes, Byzantine, 123; Gregorian, 40, 123, 227, 257; in iconography,
63, 278; rhythmic, 203, 253, 260
Modi irregulares, 203
Modus perfectus, 50
Molinier, Abbe H-J., 226
159 Molnar, Enrico C.S., "The Liturgical Reforms of John Hus,"
41 (1966):297-303
Monaulos (single pipe), 10
Monochord, 44, 173, 271
Montpellier Codex, 103
160 *Monumenta musicae byzantinae, Facsimilia & subsidia: Facsim. I:
Sticherarium,* ed. Carsten Höeg, H.J.W. Tillyard, E. Wellesz;
Sub. I, facs. 1: Handbook of the Middle Byzantine Musical Notation,
H.J.W. Tillyard; *Sub. I, facs. 2: La notation ekphonétique,* C.
Höeg. Rev: H.R. Bittermann, 11 (1936):148-50. *See 244a*
161 *Monumenta musicae byzantinae, Facsimilia, subsidia, & transcripta:
Facsim. IV: Contacarium palaeoslavicum mosquense,* A. Bugge; *Sub.
IV: Byzantine Elements in Early Slavic Chant,* M. Velimirovic;
*Transcr. VII: The Hymns of the Hirmologium, III/2: The Third Plagal
Mode,* H.J.W.Tillyard; *Transcr. VIII: The Akathistos Hymn,*
E. Wellesz; *Transcr. IX: The Hymns of the Pentecostarium,* H.J.W.
Tillyard. Rev: W. Apel, 36 (1961):643-44
162 *Monumenta musicae byzantinae, Subsidia II: Eastern Elements in
Western Chant,* E. Wellesz (*American Series I*). Rev: M. Bukofzer,
23 (1948):520-23
163 *Monumenta musicae byzantinae, Transcripta I: Die Hymnen des
Sticherarium für September,* E. Wellesz. Rev: H.R. Bittermann,
12 (1937):415
164 *Monumenta musicae byzantinae, Transcripta V: The Hymns of the Octoechus,
II,* H.J.W.Tillyard. Rev: W. Apel, 26 (1951):530-31
165 *Monumenta polyphoniae liturgicae Sanctae Ecclesiae Romanae: Ser.
I, Tom. I: Facs. I, Missa super L'homme armé,* G. Dufay; *Fasc. III,
Missa super L'homme armé,* F. Caron; *Ser. II, Tom. I: Auctorum
anonymorum Missarum Propria XVI Quorum XI Guilielmo Dufay auctori
adscribenda sunt.* Rev: W. Apel, 24 (1949): 133-36
Moon, 34
"Moor Maiden,"/Wenzel, 276
Morphology, 39
Morphology of Fifteenth Century Castilian Verse/Clarke (rev.), 57
Morris dance, 53a
Morte Arthure/Gardner (rev.), 99
Motet, 17, 18, 42, 122, 188, 199, 202, 223, 257, 260
Motet enté, 119, 188
Motets ca. 1190-1270, Complete Edition/Tischler, 104

Motetti, Guglielmi Dufay Opera Omnia/Van (rev.), 258

Motetus, 42

Mounting ligs (juga), 253

166 Mowatt, D.G., *Friderich von Hüsen, Introduction, Text, Commentary, and Glossary.* Rev: H. Heinen, 48 (1973):578-82

Mozarabe, El canto/Rojo and Prado (rev.), 212

Mozarabic chant, 142c, 179, 190, 192, 211; transcriptions, 192.
  See also Plainchant

167 "Mozarabic *Liber Ordinum*," editors' note, 3 (1928):239

Mozarabic Rite, Antiphons, Responsories and Other Chants of the/
  Brookett (rev.), 36

Müller, H., 188

168 Müller-Blattau, Wendelin, *Trouvères und Minnesänger, II: Kritische Ausgaben der Weisen, zugleich als Beitrag zu einer Melodienlehre des mittelalterlichen Liedes.* Rev: L.A. Dittmer, 32 (1957):590-93

Mummers' play, 53a

Murbacher Hymnal, 106

Muses, 227

Music, 42, 53, 95, 154, 174, 188, 201, 233a, 239, 271; and criticism,
  45, 99; edition, 83; instruction, 123, 257, 269a; power over wolves,
  204a; theorists and theory, 81, 152, 203, 233b; and verse, *see* Poetry.
  See also Transcriptions and scores

Music in the Middle Ages/Reese (rev.), 204

Music of the Spheres/Meyer-Baer (rev.), 154

Música a Catalunya fins al segle XIII/Anglès (rev.), 6

Música de las Cantigas de Santa Marta/Anglès (rev.), 7

Musica disciplina, 139

Musica ecclesiastica, 241

Musica enchiriadis, 10, 31, 42, 44, 139

Musica falsa, 119; ficta, 50, 202

Musica Guidonis, 152

Musica mensurabilis positio (Johannes de Garlandia), 271

Musical composition (intellectual purpose), 42; form, 21b; instruments,
  See Instruments; notation, *See* Notation

Musicality (of Irish and Welsh), 108

Musician-hunter, 68

Musician(s), 201, 227; animal, 1; legendary, 9, 68, 95, 252

Musik des Mittelalters und der Renaissance/Besseler (rev.), 26

Musique artificiele et naturele (Deschamps), 174

Musique au moyen âge/Gerold (rev.), 102

My lief is faren in Londe (song), 173

Mythic Drama, 151

Naker (nacaire), 69, 173

Nativity play, 50

Nato canunt (sequence), 42

Natural History (Pliny), 10

Neidhart von Ruenthal, 217, 232, 267

Nejedly, Zdenek, 163

Nelson, Alan H., 250

Nero, 201, 224

169 Nersessian, Sirarpie der, *L'illustration des psautiers grecs du moyen âge, II: Londres, Add 19.352.* Rev: G. Galaveris, 47 (1972):523-25

Oddo, Abbot, 123
Odhecaton A, Harmonice musices/Hewitt (rev.), 118
Odington, Walter, 42, 188
Odo of Cluny, 28, 39, 81, 139
Oesch, Hans (editor), 17
Office of the Hagia Sophia, 244a
Offices, 4, 16, 83, 106, 133, 238, 254, 259, 264, 280. *See also*
    Matins; Vespers
Officium pastorum (Shepherds at the manger), 238
Officium stellae (The Coming of the Magi), 238
O'Gorman, Richard (reviewer), 207
Ohlgren, Thomas H., 44
172 Ohlgren, Thomas H., "Five New Drawings in the *MS Junius II*: Their
    Iconography and Thematic Significance," 47 (1972):227-33
Oiseaux, La messe de, 206
Oktoechos, 123
Old Hall Manuscript, 272
Old Hundredth, 97
Old Hymnal, 106
Oliva, 257a
173 Olson, Clair C., "Chaucer and the Music of the Fourteenth Century,"
    16 (1941):64-91
174 Olson, Glending, "Deschamps' *Art de dictier* and Chaucer's Literary
    Environment," 48 (1973):714-23
Olwer, Nicolau d', 131
Omnis terra iubilet (antiphon), 83
Ondas do mar de vigo (Codax), 190
175 Ong, Walter J., "Wit and Mystery: a Revaluation in Mediaeval Latin
    Hymnody," 22 (1947):310-41
Onomasticon Arthurianum (Blount), 30
Onomastikon (Pollux), 10
Opera, 142, 213
Oratio Ieremiae, 211
Orbis honor celi stema (hymn), 37a
Ordinaries, 238
Ordines, 122, 188
Ordines Rachelis (Daughter of Innocents), 238
Organ, 1, 10, 27, 28, 43a, 139, 159, 173, 224
Organ: Its Evolution, Principles of Construction and Use/Sumner
    (rev.), 247
Organ of the Ancients/Farmer (rev.), 87
*Organa und mehrstimmigen Conductus in den Handschriften des deutschen
    Sprechgebiets*/Geering (rev.), 101
Organology, 69, 227
Organum, 10, 17, 42, 44, 122, 188, 203, 223, 254
Oriental music, 1
Orientis partibus (song), 16, 109
176 Orme, Nicholas, *English Schools in the Middle Ages.* Rev: K.
    Jensen, 51 (1976):524-26
Orpheus, 201
Orpheus and Eurydice, 142a
Orpheus in the Middle Ages/Friedman (rev.), 95
Orto, Marbriano de, 13

(177–183)

Osterfeiern, Die Textgeschichte der lateinischen/Boor (rev.),
   32
O'Sullivan, Jeremiah, 103
177 Ott, H. and J.M. Fletcher, eds., *The Mediaeval Statutes of the*
   Faculty of Arts of the University of Freiburg im Breisgau. Rev:
   P. Kibre, 42 (1967):181–82
Otto IV, King of Germany, 116
Ottonian air (Walther von der Vogelweide), 116
Overtones, 253
Ovid, 131
178 Owen, D.D.R., *The Evolution of the Grail Legend.* Rev: R.T.
   Pickens, 44 (1969):650–53
Owl and the Nightingale/Gardner (rev.), 99
Ox, 1
Oxford, Provençal Chansonnier/Shepard (rev.), 230
Oxford University, curriculum requirements, 81

179 Padres Benedictino de Silo, *Antiphonarium mozarabicum de la Catedral*
   de León. Rev: W.M. Whitehill, Jr., 5 (1930):231–33
180 Pächt, Otto and J.J.G. Alexander, *Illuminated Manuscripts in the*
   Bodleian Library. Rev: L.M.C. Randall, 46 (1971):533–36
Paetow, Louis J., 81, 271
Pageant, 272. *See also* Plays (secular)
Palatinalied, 260
Paléographie musicale grégorienne, Introduction à la/Suñol
   (rev.), 248
Paleography, musical, 254, 257, 271; textual, 197. *See also* 111
Palm Sunday, 213
181 Palmer, Robert B., "Bede as a Textbook Writer: a Study of his *De arte*
   metrica," 24 (1959): 573–84
Pandarus, 1
Panegyric poetry, 151a
Panegyric dictus Manlio Theodoro Consuli (Claudius Claudianus), 10
Pange lingua, 175
Panofsky, Erwin, 188
Panpipes, 173
Pantegruel (Rabelais), 91
Paolo da Firenze, 145
182 *Papers Read at the International Congress of Musicology, New York,*
   Sept. 11–16, 1939. Rev: L. Burkat, 20 (1945):359–61
Papiol, 209
Pâques en Normandie et en Angleterre, Le drame liturgique de/
   Dolan (rev.), 78
Parce continuis (sequence), 195
Parce mihi, Domine (tone recitative), 192
Parhypate, 34
Paris, Gaston, 131
Paris, Notre Dame school, 10, 122, 234; University (thirteenth century),
   271. *See also* Manuscripts
Parody, 156, 186
183 Parrish, Carl, *The Notation of Mediaeval Music.* Rev: W. Apel, 33
   (1958):427–28

188 Pirrotta, Nino, "Dante *Musicus*: Gothicism, Scholasticum, and Music,"
43 (1968):245-57
Place, Edwin B. (reviewer), 57
Plagal chants, 268a
Plainchant (plainsong), 36, 44, 83, 123, 132, 152, 227, 268a, 274.
See also Byzantine chant, Gregorian chant, Mozarabic chant
189 Plamenac, Dragan, *Johannes Ockeghem Works, Vol 2: Masses and Mass
Sections, IX-XVI.* Rev: O. Kinkeldey, 23 (1948):722-26
Planchart, Alejandro Enrique (reviewer), 36
Planctus, 254
Plato, 42, 201
Platysmation, 10
Play of Daniel, 61, 122, 238
Play of Herod, 61
Plays (sacred). *See* Dramatic ceremonies (sacred)
Plays (secular), 2, 38, 53a, 73, 121, 138a, 155, 215, 241, 280
Pleasure, 174
Plebs ergo francigena (antiphon), 83
Plectra, 1, 196
Plectral instruments. *See* Instruments, plectral
Plica, 109, 257
Pliny, the Elder, 10
Plummet writing, 37a
Pneumatic organ, 10
Pneumatica (Hero), 10
Pnigeus, 10
Poetic meters and music, 225
Poet-musicians, 174
Poetria (John of Garland), 131
Poetry, 195, 226; Castilian, 56, 190; Celtic, 256; English, 70,
99; French, 21b, 46, 220, 266; Galician, 135; Goliard, 76, 131,
277; Italian, 279; Latin, 173, 217, 226, 229; Norse, 142; Provençal,
40, 71, 233b, 237, 260; Welsh, 151a
Pollux, 10
Polyphonic music, 16, 17, 81, 119, 121, 122, 188, 233a, 257, 271;
Greek, 10; origin of, 42; singing, 241; sources of, 236
Polyphonic Music of the Fourteenth Century/Schrade (rev.), 221, 222
190 Pope, Isabel, "Mediaeval Latin Background of the Thirteenth Century
Galician Lyric," 9 (1934):3-25
Pope, Isabel (reviewer), 6, 23, 26, 66, 84, 187
191 Pope, John C., "An Unsuspected Lacuna in the Exeter Book: Divorce
Proceedings for an Ill-Matched Couple in the Old English Riddles,"
49 (1974):615-22
Popular music, 90, 119, 276. *See also* titles of specific works
Populus (congregation), 124
Porphyrius, 10
Portative organ, 173
Portugaise, Essai sur la musique religieuse, du moyen âge/Corbin
(rev.), 67
Positive organ, 173
Pōsui uestimēntum (antiphon), 211
Pothier, Joseph, 211
Poulaille, H., 90

Power, L., Missa super Alma redemptoris Mater/Documenta polyphoniae liturgicae (rev.), 77
Power, Lionel, 152
Prado, R.P. Germán, 36, 190, 212
Prado, R.P. Germán, O.S.B. *Historia del rito Mozarabe y Toledano* (rev.), 179
Prado, R.P., Germán, O.S.B. *Manual de liturgia Hispano-Visigótica o Mozárabe* (rev.), 179
192 Prado, R.P. Germán, "Mozarabic Melodics," 3 (1928):218-38
Prague University, 163
193 Pratt, Robert A., "Three Old French Sources of the Nonnes Preestes Tale (Part I)," 47 (1972):422-44
Prayers, 1
Preces (penitential song), 190, 192
Prefaces, 211
194 Preston, Raymond, "Chaucer and the Ballades Notées of Guillaume de Machaut," 26 (1951):615-23
Pribcorn (panpipes), 173
Prime, 4
Prise d'Alexandrie, La (Machaut), 173
Pro Musica (of New York), 61
Pro se suisque (responsory), 83
Procession, 16; of Palms, 213; of Prophets, 238
Processionals, 238, 264
Processions of Sarum and the Western Church/Bailey (rev.), 20
Proper chant, 152
Prophetarum (Procession of Prophets at Christmas), 238
Prophyrius, 10
Proportion, musical, 271; treatise by Chilston on, 39, 152
Proprium Sanctorum (of Silos *Antiphonary* MS 9), 211
Prosa, 42, 60, 175, 195, 234, 235
Prossas, 16
Prosula, 132
Provençal, 112; chansonnier, 230; grammar, 149; poetry, 40, 120, 233b; song, 196a, 228, 231, 260
Prudentius, 153, 192
Psalm 100, 97
Psalm 150, 139
Psalmista precipuus, 278
Psalms, 17, 133; collections of, 97; Hussite, 159, 163; singing of, 257; tones for, 36, 227
Psalms, Whole Book of (Ravenscroft), 97
Psalter, 42, 171; Aelfric, 106; Byzantine, 169; glossing, 210; illustration, 227; Lambeth, 106; Lyre Abbey, 196; Scottish metrical, 96; Utrecht, 10
Psaltery, 43a, 173, 196; sixth tone, 227
Psautiers Grecs du moyen âge, L'Illustration des/Nersessian (rev.), 169
Pseudo-Kodinos, Traité des Offices/Verpeaux (rev.), 264
Pucelle (Hours of Jeanne d'Evreux), 199
Puck (*Midsummer Night's Dream*), 1
Puer natus (trope), 86
Pueri hebraeorum (antiphon), 213
Pulse, 233a

(195–203)

Punctus, 119, 254
Pupilli facti sumus (antiphon), 192
Purification, Feast of the, 283
Puy, 18
Pythagoras, 42, 188, 201, 227

Quadrata plectra, 10
Quadrivium, 53, 81, 82, 188
Quadrupla, 223, 254
Quantas sabedes amar amigo (Codax), 190
Quatreble Sight (Power), 152
Quatuor principalia musicae (Tunstede), 50
Quem creditis natum in orbe, O Deicole (trope), 238
Quem quaeritis (trope), 238, 284
Quem quaeritis in sepulchro (trope), 155, 238, 242
Qui creavit coelum (song), 272
Qui fery (game), 199

Rabelais, François, 91
195 Raby, F.J.E., "*Amor et amicitia*: a Mediaeval Poem," 40 (1965):599–610
Rätselspiel (poem), 267
196 Ragusa, Isa, "An Illustrated Psalter from Lyre Abbey," 46 (1971):267–81
Raimbaut d'Aurenga, 40, 142b
Raimbaut d'Vaqueiras, 40
Rajput Paintings (Coomaraswamy), 278
196a Rakel, Hans-Herbert S., *Die musikalische Erscheinungsform der
Trouvèrepoesie*. Rev: M. Switten, 54 (1979): 414–16
196b Ranawake, Silvia, *Höfische Strophenkunst: Vergleichende Untersuchungen
zur Formentypologie von Minnesang und Trouvèrelied an der Wende zum
Spätmittelalter*. Rev: H. Heinen, 53 (1978):619–20
197 Rand, Edward Kennard, "A Nest of Ancient Notae," 20 (1927):160–76
198 Rand, Edward Kennard, "A Note on the Goliards," 3 (1928):595
Rand, Edward Kennard (reviewer), 56, 243
199 Randall, Lilian M.C., "Games and the Passion in Pucelle's Hours
of Jeanne d'Evreux," 47 (1972):246–57
200 Randall, Lilian M.C., *Images in the Margins of Gothic Manuscripts*.
Rev: M. Schapiro, 45 (1970):684–86
Randall, Lilian M.C. (reviewer), 180, 205
Randel, Don, 36
Ravenscroft, Thomas, *Whole Book of Psalms* (1621), 97
201 Rawski, Conrad H., "Petrarch's Dialogue on Music," 46 (1971):302–17
"Razos de Trobar" *of Raimon Vidal*/Marshall (rev.), 150
Realism, lyrics and melodies of, 79
"Realistic Observation in Twelfth Century England"/Gransden, 108
202 Reaney, Gilbert, *Guillaume de Machaut*. Rev: D.G. Hughes, 49 (1974):142–43
Rebec, 173
Recitemus per hec festa (hymn), 37a
203 Reckow, Fritz, *Der Musiktraktat des Anonymus 4. I: Edition; II:
Interpretation der Organum purum-Lehre*. Rev: D.G. Hughes,
46 (1971):536–39
Recorder, 173

Recreational singing, 81

Recte sonantia, 253

Reed (canna), 28

204 Reese, Gustave, *Music in the Middle Ages*. Rev: W. Apel, 20 (1945):119-22

Regino, Abbot of Prüm, 42, 278

Regni sedem consequentus (antiphon), 83

Regnum mundi (responsory), 83

Regulae musicae rhythmicae (Guido), 81

Regularis concordia (Winchester), 155

Regulariter indicandae, 81

Reigen (chain or ring dance), 119

Reik, T., 1

Reinach, S., 1

204a Reinhard, John R. and Vernam E. Hull, "Bran and Sceolang,"
11 (1936):42-58

Reinhard, John R. (reviewer), 230

Reinmar von Brennenberg, 217, 267

Religious Lyrics of the XIVth Century/Brown (rev.), 37

Remède de fortune (Machaut), 173

Remi of Auxerre, 103

Remigio, 188

205 Remnant, G.L., *A Catalogue of Misericords in Great Britain, with an
Essay on their Iconography by M.D. Anderson*. Rev: L.M.C. Randall,
45 (1970):159-62

*Repertorium liturgicum Augustanum. Les témoins de la liturgie du
diocèse d'Aoste*/Amiet (rev.), 4

Res glorios (Giraut de Bornelh), 233b

Responder, 119

Responsorial chant (responsories), 17, 36, 80a, 83, 122, 133, 188,
227, 238, 274

Resurrexi (Easter Introit), 86

Resurrexi et adhuc (Isaac), 284

Resurrexi et adhuc tecum sum (Introit), 278

Retourenge, 21b

Retrograde, 42

Rex gloriose (song), 97

Rex regum regis filio (responsory), 83

Rex virtutis in virtute (antiphon), 83

Reynard the Fox/Varty (rev.), 262

Rhyme, 190

Rhythm, 42, 70, 121, 188, 233a; free, 190; modal vs. declamatory, 260;
rules for, 81

206 Ribard, Jacques, ed., *Jean de Condé, La messe des oiseaux et le Dit
des Jacobins et des Fremeneurs. Edition critique.* Rev: B.S.
Merrilees, 47 (1972):111-13

207 Ribard, Jacques, *Un ménestrel de XIVe siècle: Jean de Condé.*
Rev: R. O'Gorman, 46 (1971):391-95

Ribera y Tarragó, Julian, 190

Ricercare, 145

Richard de Fournay, 260

Richard of St. Victor, 81

208 Richards, John Chatterton, "A New Manuscript of Heraclius,"
15 (1940):255-71

214 Ruelle, Pierre, *Les Congés d'Arras (Jean Bodel, Baude Fastoul, Adam de la Halle)*. Rev: W. Calen, 42 (1967):550-52

215 Rütten, Raimund, *Symbol und Mythus im altfranzösischen Rolandslied*. Rev: D. Kelly, 47 (1972):142-44

Ruggiers, Paul G. (ed. and trans.), 103

Rule, 152

Rupprecht, 267

Russia, 259, 263

Russian Church Slavonic Kannonic 1331-1332/Van der Baar (rev.), 259

Sacchetti, Franco, 147

Sachs, Curt, 69

Sackbut, 173

Sacrament, Play of the, 73`

Sacred drama. *See* Dramatic ceremonies (sacred)

Sängerkrieg, des 13. Jahrhunderts/Wachinger (rev.), 267

Sahlin, Margit R., 276

St. Aldhelm, 10, 157

St. Augustine, 10, 81, 130, 197, 198

St. Chrodegang, 96

Saint Cyrille, La Vie de/Sargologos (rev.), 218

St. Denis (monastery), 10, 96

St. Dunstan, 28, 106

St. Emmeram Anonymous, 271

St. Gall, The Abbey of, as a Centre of Literature and Art/Clark (rev.), 56

St. Gregory, 42, 96, 130, 188

St. Hugh of Cluny, 278

St. James (liturgy from Santiago de Compostela), 16

St. Jerome, 139, 271

St. John Chrysostom, 28

St. Judocus, 117

St. Lambert, 10

St. Martial of Limoges, 81, 86, 122, 254

St. Martin, Bishop of Tours, 122

St. Nicholas (play), 238

St. Stephen Harding Bible, 10

St. Victor (school), 188

216 Salazar, Adolfo, *La música en la sociedad Europea desde los primeros tiempos cristianos, Vol. 1*. Rev: L. Hibberd, 20 (1945):362-65

Salomo, Elias, 119

Saltarelli, 119

Salve Regina misericordiae, historia y leyendas/Canal (rev.), 47

Samelson, William, "Romances and Songs of the Sephardim," 120a

San Eulogio de Córdoba/Urbel (rev.), 179

San Salvador de Celanova in Galicia (monastery), 211

Sancte Iacōbe (antiphon), 211

Sangspruchdichter, Die alten Meister: Studien/Brunner (rev.), 38a

Sangspruchdichtung, 38a, 267

Sapphic verse, 190

217 Sappler, Paul, ed., *Das Königsteiner Liederbuch: Ms. germ. qu. 719 Berlin*. Rev: E. Simon, 47 (1972):340-44

Sephardim, 120a

Sequence, 4, 17, 42, 60, 83, 132, 175, 195, 234, 238, 272, 274; Easter, 175; nonliturgical, 235; sources, 235

Serranilla, 131

Serventois, 18

Service book, 55

228 Sesini, Ugo, *Le melodie trobadoriche nel canazoniere Provenzale della Biblioteca Ambrosiana R. 71 Sup.* Rev: M. Bukofzer, 23 (1948):506-7

229 Sesini, Ugo, *Poesia e musica nella latinita cristiana dal III al X secolo.* Rev: E. Gianturco, 27 (1952):250-54

Sesquialtera, 271

Sesquitertia, 271

Seven, Leuthold von, 267

Seven trumpets, 151

Sext, 16

Shawms, 69, 173, 196; (fourth & eighth tone), 43a, 227

230 Shepard, William Pierce, *The Oxford Provençal Chansonnier: Diplomatic Edition of the Manuscript of the Bodleian Library Douce 269.* Rev: J.R. Reinhard, 3 (1928):608-11

231 Shepard, William Pierce, "Two Derivative Songs by Aimeric de Pequilhan," 2 (1927):296-309

Shepherd, Massey H., Jr. (reviewer), 47, 133, 185

Shepherds' Play, 233

Shofar (ram's horn), 1

Shrewsbury Music (play), 73

Shrovetide, 155

Shuttle, 191

Si ascendero in caelum (antiphon), 192

Si je me plains (song), 90

Sight, 152; sight singing, 269a

Signal instruments, 69

Silenus, 1

Silos, 211; *Antiphonarium*, 179; *Liber Ordinum*, 192

232 Simon, Eckehard, *Neidhart von Ruental.* Rev: P.W. Tax, 52 (1977):1046-48

Simon, Eckehard (reviewer), 124, 155, 217, 238, 280

Simplices, 254

233 Sinanglow, Leah, "The Christ Child as Sacrifice: A Medieval Tradition and the Corpus Christi Plays," 48 (1973):491-509

Singenberg, Ulrich von, 267

Singing, extemporized, 145, 148, 241; with eyes closed, 193; festive, 241; heavenly, 188; off pitch, 257; Orpheus, 142a; part, 152; ranges, 21b; recreational, 81; schools, 139; from the *Sticherarion*, 163, 164, 218

233a Siraisi, Nancy G., "The Music of Pulse in the Writings of Italian Academic Physicians (Fourteenth and Fifteenth Centuries)," 50 (1975):689-710

Sirens' song, 9, 201

Sirventes, 54, 142b, 209

Sistrum, 1

Sitientes (Introit), 192

Skårup, Poul (reviewer), 150

Slavic music, 161, 259

Slide trumpets, 69

Smith, Cyril S., 253
233b Smith, Nathaniel B., *Figures of Repetition in the Old Provençal Lyric: A Study in the Style of the Troubadours*. Rev: F. Goldin, 53 (1978):848-51
Smith, Nathaniel B. (reviewer), 21a, 170, 268a, 269a, 270a
Smith, William Sheppard, 272
Smits van Waesberghe, Joseph. *See* Waesberghe, Joseph van
Smoldon, W.L., 132, 242, 250
Sociedad Europea, La musica en, desde los primeros tiempos cristianos/ Salazar (rev.), 216
Socrates, 201
Soldanieri, Nicolo, 147
Soldiers' Song of Modena, 219
Solesmes Antiphonary, 211
Solmisation, 257
Solo vs. choral music, 272
Sonetto, 147
Song, 9, 16, 21, 201, 217, 223, 272; Cambridge, 131, 244; crusader's, 186; drinking, 241; Eddic, 142; French, 21b; German, 124; Goliard, 198, 277; Ladino, 120a; Latin, 280; popular, 276; Provençal,142c, 231; Soldiers of Modena, 219; Welsh, 151a. *See also* Chanson
Song of Roland, 80, 126, 215, 220
Song of Solomon, 272
Song of Songs, 272
Song of the Ass, 1, 109
Song or reading schools, 176
Songfest (cantares), 273
Sonnets (Petrarch), 279
Sottes chanson, 18
*Sottes chansons, Deux recueils de, et Bibliothèque Nationale Fr. 24432/*Langfors (rev.), 140
Souvent souspere (chanson), 119
Space, 152
Spain, 5-7, 56, 120a, 188, 190
234 Spanke, Hans, "Ein unveröffentlichtes lateinisches Liebeslied," 5 (1930):431-33
235 Spanke, Hans, "Zur Geschichte der lateinischen nichtliturgischen Sequenz," 7 (1932):367-82
Specie tua (Gradual), 278
Speculative thinking (medieval music), 42
Spervogel, 267
236 Spiess, Lincoln B., "An Introduction to the Pre-St. Martial Practical Sources of Early Polyphony," 22 (1947):16-17
Spiritus et alme (trope), 42
Spitzer, Leo, 53
237 Spitzer, Leo, *L'amour lointain de Jaufrē Rudel et le sens de la poesie des troubadours*. Rev: A.R. Nykl, 20 (1945):252-58
Sponsus (play), 61
Square notation, 203
Stabat Mater dolorosa, 79, 175
*Stag of Love: The Chase/*Thiébaux (rev.), 251
Stampjan, 119
Stanley, E.G., 106

Theoretical topics, 268a; arithmetical, 270a; English treatises on, 39, 152; Spanish, 257a; table of, 81

Theorists, 81, 151. *See also* names of individuals

Thibaud de Navarre, 260

Thibault, Geneviève, 223

251 Thiébaux, Marcelle, *The Stag of Love: The Chase in Medieval Literature.* Rev: J.H. Fisher, 52 (1977):437-39

Third, 152

Thirteenth, 152

252 Thomas, J.W., *Tannhäuser: Poet and Legend. With Texts and Translations of his Works.* Rev: H. Heinen, 52 (1977):439-42

Thomasin, 267

253 Thompson, Daniel V., "Theophilus Presbyter: Words and Meaning in Technical Translation," 42 (1967):313-39

Thompson, Lawrence S. (reviewer), 138

Thurot, C., 226

Tibia, 201

Tibynus, Nicholaus, 271

Tillyard, H.J.W., *Handbook of the Middle Byzantine Musical Notation/ Monumenta musicae byzantinae* (rev.), 160

Tillyard, H.J.W., *The Hymns of the Hirmologium, the Third Plagal Mode/Monumenta musicae byzantinae* (rev.), 161

Tillyard, H.J.W., *The Hymns of the Octoechus/Monumenta musicae byzantinae* (rev.), 164

Tillyard, H.J.W., *The Hymns of the Pentecostarium/Monumenta musicae byzantinae* (rev.), 161

Tillyard, H.J.W., ed., *Sticherarium/Monumenta musicae byzantinae* (rev.), 160

Timbrel, 173

Tinctoris, Johannes, 13, 201

254 Tischler, Hans, "New Historical Aspects of the Parisian Organa," 25 (1950):21-35

Tischler, Hans (editor), 194; (reviewer), 16, 260; (subject), 188

Tittel (author), 139

Toccata, 145

Töne, 38a

Ton y Brenhin (song), 97

Tonaires, Inventaire, analyse, comparaison./Huglo (rev.), 123

Tonary, 123, 227, 268a

Tones (plainsong), in iconography, 63, 278

Topographicia Hibernica, 108

255 Topsfield, L.T., *Troubadours and Love.* Rev: H.S.F. Collins, 52 (1977):750-51

Tornada, 119, 226

Totenfeier (poem), 267

Tournai Mass, 13

Tous les regretz (chanson), 90

Towneley Cycle, 50, 151, 233, 238

Transcriptions and scores. (Here follows a list of music examples, including facsimiles, photographs, and other copies. Not all pieces are complete.)

Ad te Deus meus (antiphon), 83

272 Wall, Carolyn, "York Pageant XLVI and Its Music" with a "Note on the
   Transcriptions" by Ruth Steiner, 46 (1971):689-712
273 Waller, Martha S., "The Physician's Tale: Geoffrey Chaucer and Fray
   Juan Garcia de Castrojerez," 51 (1976):292-306
   Walther von der Vogelweide, 116, 260, 267
   Walther von der Vogelweide/Kraus (rev.), 136
   Wamba, Antiphonary of, 179, 190, 192
   Waterhouse, Osborn, 73
   Wayte pipe, 173
   Weavers Guild, 272
274 Wegner, Gunter, *Kirchenjahr und Messfeier in der Würzburger
   Domliturgie des späten Mittelalters*. Rev: R. Pfaff, 47 (1972):151-52
   Weinert, W., 1
   Weiss, Gunther, 86
   Wellendorffer, 201
   Wellesz, Egon, *The Akathistos Hymn/Monumenta musicae byzantinae*
   (rev.), 161
   Wellesz, Egon, *Eastern Elements in Western Chant/Monumenta musicae
   byzantinae* (rev.), 162
275 Wellesz, Egon, *A History of Byzantine Music and Hymnography*, 2d Ed.
   Rev: K.J. Levy, 27 (1962):467-69
   Wellesz, Egon, *Die Hymnen des Sticherarium für September/Monumenta
   musicae byzantinae* (rev.), 163
   Wellesz, Egon, ed., *Sticherarium/Monumenta musicae byzantinae*
   (rev.), 160
   Welsh meter, song, and tales, 151a, 178
276 Wenzel, Siegfried, "The Moor Maiden - A Contemporary View,"
   49 (1974):69-74
   Wenzel, Siegfried (reviewer), 110a
277 Whicher, George F., *The Goliard Poets: Mediaeval Latin Songs and
   Satires*. Rev: E.C. Evans, 26 (1951):425-27
278 Whitehill, Walter Muir, Jr., "Gregorian Capitals from Cluny,"
   2 (1927):385-95
   Whitehill, Walter Muir, Jr. (reviewer), 179, 212, 248
   Wido, 131
   Wierschin, Martin W. (reviewer), 267
   Wilhelm, J.J. (reviewer), 120
   Wilhelm of Hirsau, 208
279 Wilkins, Ernest Hatch, "Petrarch's First Collection of his Italian
   Poems," 7 (1932):169-80
   Wilkins, Nigel, 174
   William I, Count (1304-1337), 206
   William of Conches, 271
   William of Malmesbury, 10, 52
   Williams, Arnold (reviewer), 114
   Williams, C.F. Abdy, 10
   Wilson, Evelyn Faye, 271
280 Wimmer, Ruprecht, *Deutsch und Latein im Osterspiel: Untersuchungen
   zu den volkssprachlichen Entsprechungstexten der lateinschen
   Strophenlieder*. Rev: E. Simon, 52 (1977):451-54
   Winchester organ, 10
   Winchester Troper, 122
   Wind instruments. *See* Instruments, wind

Wolf, Johannes, 119
Wolfram von Eschenbach, 1, 267
Wolkenstein, Oswald von, 244a
Woolley, C. Leonard, 1
Wright, Edith A. (reviewer), 74
Wright, W.C., 10
Württemberg, Count Heinrich von, 217
Würzburger Domliturgie, Kirchenjahr und Messfeier in der/Wegner
   (rev.), 274
Wulstan, 10
Wyclif, John, 159
Wylde, John, 152

Y̆ ondas que eu vin (Codax), 190
281 Yasser, Joseph, *Mediaeval Quartal Harmony*. Rev: L. Ellingwood,
   15 (1940):127-28
Yerushalmi, Yosef Hayim (reviewer), 120a
York hymnal, 106; pageant, 272; play, 233
282 Young, Karl, *The Drama of the Mediaeval Church*. Rev: G.R. Coffman,
   9 (1934):109-17. *See also* 32, 238
283 Young, Karl, "Dramatic Ceremonies of the Feast of the Purification,"
   5 (1930):97-102
284 Young, Karl, "The Home of the Easter Play," 1 (1926):71-86
284a Young, Karl, "Instructions for Parish Priests," 11 (1936):224-31

Zain, Cadidiṓres (lesson of nocturn), 211
Zamorensis, Aegidius, 81
Zarlino, 201
Zetus, 201
Ziegler, Vickie L., *The Leit Word in Minnesang*, 233b
Zumthor, Paul, 196a
Zweter, Reinmar von, 267